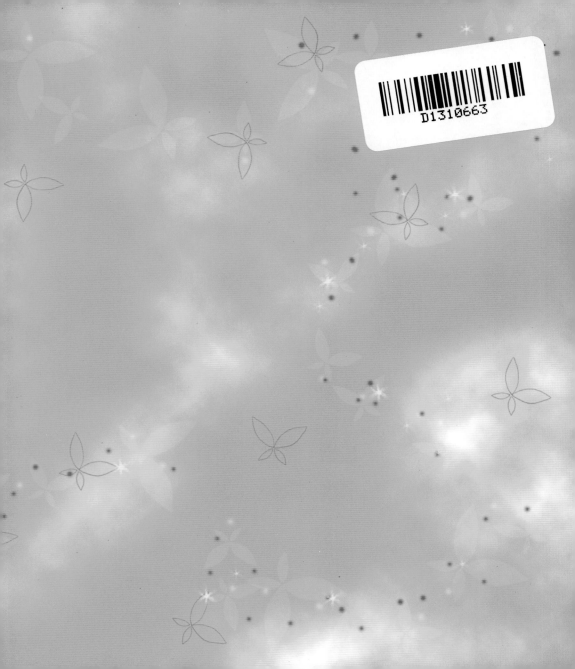

ISBN: 978-0-545-20249-7

First published in Great Britian by Orchard Books U. K. in 2008.

12 11 10 9 8 7 6 5 4 3 2   10 11 12 13 14 15/0
53

New Material Only   Matériaux neufs seulement
Reg. No. 06T-1710609   N° de permis 06T-1710609
Content: Contenu:
Polyurethane Foam   Mousse de polyuréthane

Printed in China
First Scholastic Printing, January 2010

My RAINBOW magic™

Birthday Secrets

Dear Rainbow Magic Friend,

We were so excited when we found out that the fairies were ready to share their birthday secrets with you. The fairies love birthdays so much, they even have their own special party workshop!

This book is filled with fantastic ideas for birthday fun and games, plus a Rainbow Magic fairyscope for everyone!

Lots of love,

Kirsty and Rachel XOXO

Based on the books by
Daisy Meadows

Scholastic Inc.

New York   Toronto   London   Auckland
Sydney   Mexico City   New Delhi   Hong Kong

January

January is a month of new beginnings and New Year magic!

1st-12th
Crystal the Snow Fairy
New year, new birthday! Early January birthday girls are gentle, just like snowflakes. Make a resolution to try some new things this year. You'll be surprised at what you can do!

13th-22nd
Isabelle the Ice Dance Fairy
You're a graceful girl – just like me! This year, make plenty of plans with your friends to tell stories and learn new dance routines. Sharing is lots of fun!

23rd-31st
Scarlett the Garnet Fairy
You always sparkle and dazzle, no matter what the weather! When your birthday comes, put on your brightest dress. Your friends will love partying with you today and all year long!

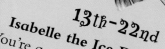

Birthstone
Scarlett's beautiful red garnet comes from Queen Titania's magic tiara. It is the gemstone for all January birthdays.

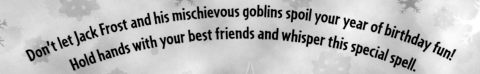

Don't let Jack Frost and his mischievous goblins spoil your year of birthday fun!
Hold hands with your best friends and whisper this special spell.

No icy finger,
No frozen stare,
No naughty goblins
anywhere,
All the fairies sing
their song,
Chilly Jack Frost
now be gone!

February

February is a time for sipping hot chocolate and swapping Valentine's cards with friends!

1st-12th
Amy the Amethyst Fairy
Girls born at the start of February are kindhearted, honest, and true. Dream up some thrilling new adventures this year to show your friends that you can be full of surprises, too.

13th-22nd
Juliet the Valentine Fairy
You're a friendly person with a wonderful imagination and a sparkling mind. Don't be too shy to share your ideas—when you talk, people listen!

23rd-29th
Louise the Lily Fairy
The year ahead is going to be full of all kinds of excitement! Paint pictures, take photos, and write poems to remember all these magical experiences.

Birthstone
Amy is very proud of the way her deep purple jewel glows in the light. Amethyst is the special birthstone for girls born in February.

A Caring Card

Valentine's Day is all about celebrating special friendships. Why not make this pretty Valentine's card for your closest friend?

You will need:
- White paper
- Pencil
- Scissors
- Felt-tip markers or crayons

1 Take a sheet of paper and fold it neatly in half. Press down along the fold and then open the sheet again.

2 Flatten the paper in front of you, then use a pencil to draw a heart. Make sure that the top half of the heart sits above the folded line and the other half below the line.

3 Ask a grown-up to help you very carefully cut around the top half of the heart. Only cut out the parts of the heart that appear above the fold line.

4 Fold the card flat again, then use your favorite markers or crayons to color the heart in.

5 When you've finished coloring, fold the card back along the crease again. Your beautiful heart will pop up at the top!

Try using glittery gel pens or adding stickers to create extra sparkle!

March

Blow away the winter cobwebs— magical March has arrived!

1st–12th
Abigail the Breeze Fairy
Energetic and lively—you're full of the joys of spring! You've got so much to do and say this year, but make sure to give your friends the chance to keep up with you.

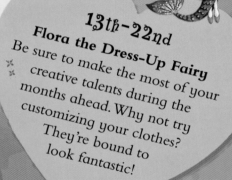

13th–22nd
Flora the Dress-Up Fairy
Be sure to make the most of your creative talents during the months ahead. Why not try customizing your clothes? They're bound to look fantastic!

23rd–31st
Bella the Bunny Fairy
Your special connection with animals comes as no surprise—you're such a caring person! It's fine to let others lead the way, but make time to do the things that you enjoy this year, too.

Birthstone
Aquamarine is the stone for all March birthdays. This pretty stone is the color of the ocean on a sunny day!

Fun Day Destiny!

Do you know what day of the week you were born? Check with your mom or dad, then find out which Fun Day Fairy watches over your special day.

Megan
the Monday Fairy

Tara
the Tuesday Fairy

Willow
the Wednesday Fairy

Thea
the Thursday Fairy

Felicity
the Friday Fairy

Sienna
the Saturday Fairy

Sarah
the Sunday Fairy

Don't forget to ask your best friend when she was born, too! You might share the same Fun Day Fairy....

Kirsty and Rachel
xoxo

April

April days are full of baby animals, green fields, and spring showers!

1st–12th
Hayley the Rain Fairy
April birthday girls love trying new things, and sign up for all sorts of clubs and hobbies. Try not to say yes to everything, through— we all need to rest sometimes!

13th–22nd
Polly the Party Fun Fairy
You take center stage at every party—all your friends adore your jokes and giggles. Experiment with rainbow colors this year—the change is sure to suit you!

23rd–30th
Lucy the Diamond Fairy
You're a born leader, always the first to take charge when your friends don't know what to do. Your courage this year will lead you to an unexpected place and some exciting news!

Birthstone
Lucy's precious diamond reflects spinning rainbows in the sunlight. Diamond is the jewel for all April birthdays.

Perfect Parties!

The Party Fairies love planning birthday parties! There is always lots to do, so they use this checklist to make sure that everything runs smoothly.

Check first with a grown-up to see if you can have a party and how many friends you're allowed to invite!

Make party bags filled with stickers and little treats.

Send invitations in plenty of time. Handmade ones are always special, and less expensive, too. Don't forget to write "RSVP" on each one!

Plan your party food and drinks. Small treats are easiest, leaving your friends free to chat and have fun!

Gather together all the things that you will need for party games, plus any prizes you'd like to give out.

Treat yourself to bubble bath an hour or so before the party starts. This way, you'll be relaxed when your guests arrive!

Put together a pretty party outfit, then add the accessories that will look just right.

Think about the music you are going to play and the decorations you'd like to put up.

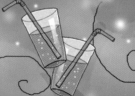

May

Merry May is the month for warm weather wishes and garden games!

1st-12th

Fern the Green Fairy

These birthday girls are warm and welcoming, just like the first May sunbeams! You're sure to share some wonderful times with friends this year.

13th-22nd

Charlotte the Sunflower Fairy

When it comes to making an impression, you're head and shoulders above the rest. Make sure to let your friends share the limelight, too!

23rd-31st

Emily the Emerald Fairy

You're a real chatterbox, always bursting with the latest happenings, gossip, and stories. Why not make a pen pal this year, so you can swap news with someone far away?

Birthstone

Emily uses her emerald to see the future in pools. This May birthstone flickers and glows a deep sea-green.

Petal Personality!

At this time of the year, the Petal Fairies are busy making their blooms beautiful for summertime! Answer the questions in this flowchart to find out which flowery fairy you're most like.

Are you a do-er or a dreamer?

Do-er → **Are you happiest alone or in a crowd?**

Dreamer → **Do you prefer fun fashion or old favorites?**

Alone → **Do you prefer to be a trendsetter or everyone's friend?**

Crowd → **Are you happiest center stage or behind-the-scenes?**

Fashion → **Is your style classic or funky?**

Faves → **Do you like garden games or country walks?**

Trendsetter → **Hot-house flower**

Friend → **Big-hearted bloom**

Stage → **Rare beauty**

Behind → **Queen of the garden**

Classic → **Ray of sunshine**

Funky → **Super in scarlet**

Games → **Flowery friend**

Walks → **Blushing bud**

Olivia the Orchid Fairy
An eye-catching beauty who always attracts a crowd!

Pippa the Poppy Fairy
A kind and caring team player – stunning both inside and out.

Ella the Rose Fairy
Sometimes shy, but blessed with natural grace and sweetness.

Danielle the Daisy Fairy
The good-hearted girl-next-door who everybody loves to love!

June

Sunny June days are perfect for sharing ripe strawberries and sweet homemade lemonade!

1st-12th
Ruby the Red Fairy
These birthday girls should get close to nature this year. Secrets swapped with friends in a fairy ring at the bottom of a summer garden will give you some unforgettable memories!

13th-22nd
India the Moonstone Fairy
You're a dreamer—your head is often in the clouds! Use your amazing imagination to write stories, poems, and plays in the months ahead.

23rd-30th
Phoebe the Fashion Fairy
Your cute fashion sense always turns heads. Why not try customizing your own clothes this year? Your fab style could work wonders with an old necklace or forgotten T-shirt!

Birthstone
India's moonstone glows with all the colors of the rainbow. Girls born in June are very lucky to have such a magical birthstone!

Wishing Wand

Every Rainbow Magic fairy has an enchanted wand! Here's how to make your own signature wand—all you need are nimble fingers and a mind for magic.

You will need:
- Newspapers
- A wooden chopstick
- Poster paint
- Paintbrush
- Thin satin ribbon
- Scissors
- Spray adhesive
- Glitter

1. Lay out some old newspapers, then paint the chopstick a pretty color.

2. When the chopstick has dried, pick out a length of satin ribbon.

3. Wrap the ribbon up and down the wand. Start from the wide end of the chopstick and leave 8 inches of ribbon (a). When you wind the ribbon back to the base, leave another 8 inches extra before tying the ends in a bow (b).

4. Ask a grown-up to lightly cover the entire wand in spray adhesive.

5. Sprinkle glitter up and down the length of the wand and shake off the excess. Your sparkly wand is ready to dazzle your friends!

Why not try adding to your wand? Stick-on silk flowers, strings of beads and sequins, or a star shape will all look beautiful!

July

Welcome to July, a month for wonderful weekends and poolside fun!

1st-12th
Goldie the Sunshine Fairy
You're as bright as a sunbeam —no one can resist all the kind and thoughtful things you do. This year, it's your turn to be treated, as your friends show you just how much you mean to them, too!

13th-22nd
Penny the Pony Fairy
You love the thrill of adventure —life is a rollercoaster whenever you're in charge! Slow down this year; it's nice to take things easy some of the time!

23rd-31st
Lauren the Puppy Fairy
If you're not allowed to have the pet you've always wished for, don't worry! Volunteer to care for the school hamster or help friends look after their animals— you're destined to make a pet pal.

Birthstone
The ruby is the birthstone for all those born in July. The ruby is often associated with power and confidence!

Animal Magic!

Did you know that the year you were born doesn't just tell you your age? The Chinese zodiac features 12 animals, each with their own character types. Use this chart to find the animal for your birth year!

Rat	1996	Dragon	2000	Monkey	2004
Ox	1997	Snake	2001	Rooster	2005
Tiger	1998	Horse	2002	Dog	2006
Rabbit	1999	Sheep	2003	Pig	2007

Rat
You're a bright spark who's always up for fun! You're popular and kind.

Ox
Trustworthy and honest, ox girls always protect the ones they love!

Tiger
You're generous and a wonderful hostess – tigers throw great parties!

Rabbit
You're sweet, shy, and very popular, although you often don't know it!

Dragon
Don't be scared of the dragon! Under your fiery exterior lies a heart of gold.

Snake
You're a thoughtful girl and like to take your time. You are lovable and bright.

Horse
Horses love roaming far and wide, spreading sunshine as they go!

Sheep
You have a magical imagination and are very gentle and trustworthy.

Monkey
You're a sociable party princess and love to share funny stories and silly jokes.

Rooster
Roosters are practical and observant. You are a loyal friend!

Dog
You're patient and kind, and make an amazing best friend!

Pig
You adore pretty things and share them with your many friends!

August

1st–12th
Sky the Blue Fairy
Whether on vacation with best friends or staying closer to home, you're always cheerful and bright. There will be all kinds of smiley surprises in the year ahead!

13th–22nd
Kylie the Carnival Fairy
My birthday girls love dressing in dazzling costumes and soaking up the limelight. This year, try helping out backstage, too—you might just discover some impressive hidden talents!

23rd–31st
Joy the Summer Vacation Fairy
When you're around, it feels like the sun is shining, even when the weather outside is dreary! August birthday girls enjoy starting new collections, so what about seashells?

Birthstone
The peridot is the birthstone for August. A stunning green color, this is often used in pretty jewelery.

Magical Masks

If you're having a birthday party this month, why not ask your guests to create and wear their own magical masks? Or you could make these together at the party!

You will need:
- Colored paper
- Pencil
- Scissors
- Felt-tip markers
- Sequins
- Glue
- Ribbon

1. On a piece of paper, draw a face outline that is slightly bigger than your own.

2. Cut the shape out and hold it up to your face, then mark where the eyes should go. Ask a grown-up to carefully snip out almond-shaped eyeholes.

3. Hold the mask back up to your face, then sketch where the nose sits. Now carefully cut off the bottom half of the mask so that your mouth becomes visible.

4. Use your brightest felt-tip markers to decorate the mask with hearts, butterflies, and stars.

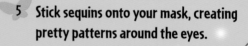

5. Stick sequins onto your mask, creating pretty patterns around the eyes.

6. Make a small hole on either side of the fairy mask.

7. Thread a long piece of ribbon through one of the holes and tie it in a knot at the back of the mask. Repeat on the other side, then tie the ends together behind your head.

8. Take the mask off, then ask a grown-up to curl the ribbon ends with the scissors.

September

September's the month to play with school friends in the hazy autumn sunshine!

1st-12th
Sunny the Yellow Fairy
September girls are team players! If you're not a sports star yet, maybe you haven't found the right game for you. Why not try having fun on a basketball court or taking on a ping-pong match?

13th-22nd
Katie the Kitten Fairy
A purr-fect afternoon for you is snuggling on a cozy sofa with a chocolate bar and a girly DVD. Why not invite a friend next time? Chilling on your own is fun, but friend-time is twice as nice!

23rd-30th
Sophie the Sapphire Fairy
When your friends get in a fight, they turn to you. You're a calm, lovable peacemaker with a special knack of turning frowns upside down! Keep up the good work and you'll soon be the most popular girl in town!

Birthstone
A fountain of blue sparkles flash around Sophie's stunning sapphire. This September birthstone is a gorgeous glittery gem.

Furry Friends

Pets have birthdays, too! Every year, Katie has a special birthday party in Fairyland for her kitten, Shimmer. The other Pet Fairies come over to help her celebrate—and they bring their pets!

Draw a picture here of your pet, or a pet that you dream of owning. Don't forget to write their name and fill in their birthday if you know it!

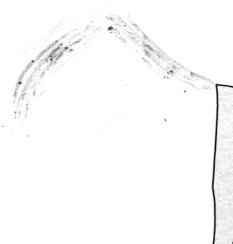

Name:..Stacey....

Birthday:..............

Kirsty's kitten, Pearl, is still young, but when her birthday comes around, the Tate family is going to sign a special card! Kittens don't like birthday cake, so she'll have a yummy cat treat from the pet shop, instead!

Kirsty and Rachel xoxo

October

Crisp October days are perfect for dressing up, apple-bobbing, and lighting Halloween pumpkins!

1st–12th
Amber the Orange Fairy
You're a busy, busy birthday girl! You've got so much going on, friends never know whether you're coming or going. Sit back and relax from time to time this year, and let everyone else catch up!

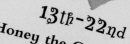

13th–22nd
Honey the Candy Fairy
If there's someone in your class you've always wanted to make friends with, this is the year to walk over and say hello. Chances are they've been feeling a little bit shy, too!

23rd–31st
Trixie the Halloween Fairy
Your birthday might be near Halloween, but you're not the least bit spooky! In fact, all your friends would say that you're the most helpful girl they know. Your kindness will be rewarded this year.

Birthstone
The sparkly opal is the birthstone for all October birthdays. The stone is said to enhance imagination!

Perfect Party Bags!

At the end of a birthday party, Honey loves to give out mini party bags to all her Rainbow Magic friends!

You will need:
- Sheets of cellophane in different colors
- Dinner plate
- Ballpoint pen
- Scissors
- Saucer
- Tissue paper
- Fairy trinkets
- Small elastic band
- Glue
- Sequins
- Ruler
- Satin ribbon
- Beads

1 Gather three sheets of cellophane in at least two different colors. Lay a dinner plate over the top and draw around the edge in ballpoint pen. Cut out the circle and set it aside.

2 Lay a saucer on a double layer of tissue paper and draw around the edge.

3 Cut out the circle of tissue and lay it in the middle of the cellophane. Place one or two fairy trinkets in the center, such as a sparkly hair clip, a sticker, or even a handwritten spell!

4 Draw together all the edges of the circle, then slip a small elastic band over the top to form a bag. Fan out the layers.

5 Stick sequins over the bag so that it shimmers in the light.

6 Measure out a length of ribbon at least 8 inches long. Thread two or three beads on each end and secure in place with a knot.

7 Tie the beaded ribbon over the elastic band with a neat bow.

November

As the days get chilly and the nights frost over, November arrives with lots of fairy fun!

1st-12th
Evie the Mist Fairy
My birthday girls are both magical and mysterious. Even the people that you are closest to never quite know what you're up to! Don't keep everything to yourself, however, or you might miss out.

13th-22nd
Chloe the Topaz Fairy
You're not afraid to stand up for the things that you believe in, on your birthday or any other day of the year! In the months ahead, your fairy good values will be cherished by those around you.

23rd-30th
Cherry the Cake Fairy
Friends adore your kooky fashion sense and funny ways—you're sweet enough to eat! Make sure you stay true to your own style, and before you know it everyone will be copying you.

Birthstone
Chloe's precious topaz glows a fiery orange—it's the perfect gemstone for all November birthday girls!

Spells for Smiling!

Whenever the fairies want to make someone smile, they wave their wands and create a happiness spell. Copy this one onto a piece of paper and pass it to a friend who needs cheering up!

To my friend so dear and true,
A Rainbow Magic wish for you:
Happy times, joy, and care,
Shall follow you everywhere!
Fairy giggles, fun and laughter,
And a happy ever after,
May your days be
filled with glee,
For you have given
these to me!

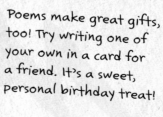

Poems make great gifts, too! Try writing one of your own in a card for a friend. It's a sweet, personal birthday treat!

Kirsty and Rachel XOXO

December

December brings snow, snuggly nights, and warm holiday wishes!

1st-12th
Inky the Indigo Fairy
You're a first-class birthday planner, with all sorts of fairy-tastic ideas! When an exciting new school project is suggested this year, put your hand up—you're just the girl to do a great job!

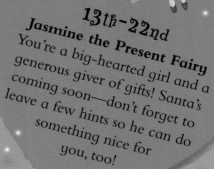

13th-22nd
Jasmine the Present Fairy
You're a big-hearted girl and a generous giver of gifts! Santa's coming soon—don't forget to leave a few hints so he can do something nice for you, too!

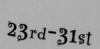

23rd-31st
Holly the Christmas Fairy
When it comes to fabulous festive birthdays, you take the cake! Your happy outlook will bring you lots of love and luck—for the new year and beyond!

Birthstone
The turquoise birthstone is the color of a bright summer sky! This stone is said to enhance creativity.

Perfect Presents

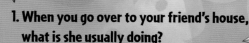

Choosing a present for your best friend can be really tricky. Answer these quiz questions, then check your answers to help you decide on the perfect fairy gift.

1. When you go over to your friend's house, what is she usually doing?
a. Curled up with a book
b. Sorting out her wardrobe
c. Playing with her pet

2. What sort of party is your best friend most likely to have?
a. Dress-up
b. Dance
c. Picnic at a petting zoo

3. What posters are on your friend's bedroom wall?
a. The latest music sensation
b. Pages from fashion magazines
c. Cute baby animals

4. What does she like to do on a Saturday afternoon?
a. Go to the movies
b. Head to the mall
c. Do a craft

Mostly As
Seems like your friend's an imaginative girl with a head full of fantasies and happy ever afters! Why not get her . . .

* The latest installment of her favorite book series
* A pretty notepad or journal
* A DVD of her fave film

Mostly Bs
Your best friend is a fashion diva, completely crazy about clothes! She would love . . .

* A set of twinkly barettes
* A friendship bracelet or locket
* A cute hat or scarf

Mostly Cs
Your friend adores animals, just like the Pet Fairies! How about presenting her with . . .

* A helpful pet-care book
* A photo frame
* A little animal ornament for her bedroom

More magical fairy fun!

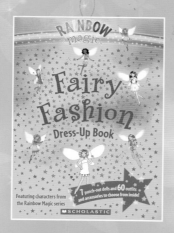

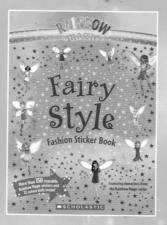